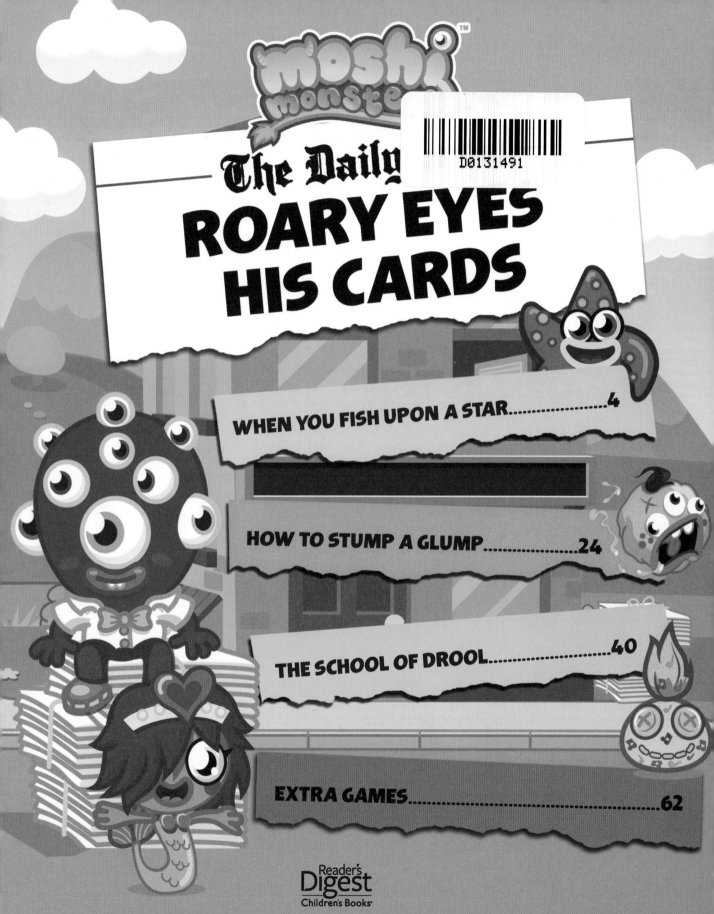

Moshi Monsters™

The Daily
ROARY EYES
HIS CARDS

Reader's Digest
Children's Books®

New York, New York • Montréal, Québec • Bath, United Kingdom

D0131491

The Daily Growl

WHEN YOU FISH UPON A STAR

Ace Reporter Loses Eye, Finds a Heap of Adventure

You wouldn't believe what I saw down at The Port! No, not Gail Whale doing cannonballs into Potion Ocean, I saw my pal Fumble, and she was on her way to see Elder Furi. And you know me, I can't say no to a good adventure, so I went with her! We trekked through the Screamington Swamp, camped up at Stumpy Peak with some friends, and even got to help out with the Moshling Boshling tournament.

FREE ROX!

What's the name of Avril LeScream and Riff Sawfinger's band? The answer is your secret code, but remember do not use spaces!

2

HOW TO STUMP A GLUMP

Glumps Try to Trump Monstro City, Get Thumped Instead

Things are never quite as they seem when Glumps are on the loose. This was the case on that fateful day the Glumps were fed Smart Tarts and became smarter and more trouble than they'd ever been before! As they wreaked havoc on the shops in Monstro City, my shopkeeper pals and I banded together to outsmart the new and improved Glumps. Just another day of keeping Monstro City free from the clutches of CLONC.

THE SCHOOL OF DROOL

Beanie Blob Slogger Slogs Last Blob

Sometimes an ordinary day at work turns out to be something EXTRAordinary. Especially when you meet a green-haired Zommer who has a ROCKIN' hidden talent. It can be a truly transforming experience! With a little help from Avril Le Scream and Riff Sawfinger, The School of Drool became The School of Cool.

WHEN YOU FISH UPON A STAR

I was having a stroll over at The Port searching for my missing eye, when I heard something. *Oomph, thunk, splat!* It was Fumble the Acrobatic SeaStar. She'd tripped over her star-tip and face-planted in the sand.

"Are you alright?" I asked, helping Fumble up.

"Sure, I guess," she replied sadly, dusting sand off of herself. I noticed she was carrying a bag. It looked like she was going on a trip.

"Where are you headed with that bag full of stuff?" I asked.

"I've had enough of being laughed at for being the clumsiest of all the Moshlings! I'm off to find Elder Furi. You see, I heard he could help me learn to be more graceful. After all, he IS the wisest monster in Monstro City."

"Wow! But Elder Furi hangs out all the way over at the volcano and that's a LONG way to go." Fumble looked so pitiful. I knew she was an Acrobatic SeaStar, but I guess I'd forgotten that she's also SUPER clumsy. I'd be pretty fed up too!

"I know, I know. But I've been planning this trip for weeks," she said, as she put the stuff that spilled from her pack back in her bag. I noticed she had Star-Tip Glue, a jar of Octopus Spit, and a deck of cards.

"Do you want some company?" I asked. "I have the whole weekend off of work, and I doubt Tyra Fangs will miss me. There's a Monstro City's Next Top Model marathon on and she won't even notice I'm gone."

Fumble's eyes crinkled in a smile. "I'd love it, Roary!" she exclaimed.

"I should probably find my missing eye, first." I said. "Have you seen it? There's nothing worse than not knowing where they all are. It gives me a feeling of emptiness."

"I think I can help you," she offered. "I'm pretty sure I saw a school of Batty Bubblefish playing with an eyeball down in Potion Ocean. Let's go!"

Splash! We jumped off the dock and into the crystal blue water. Before long, we caught up to Blurp, a Batty Bubblefish. He was swimming upside down!

"Why are you swimming upside down, Blurp?" I asked.

"Hello there, purple stranger!" he bubbled. "Sometimes I forget which way is up. Oops," he said as he flipped right-side up.

"That's Roary Scrawl, silly!" Fumble said. "You've met him like a MILLION times."

"Oh, right, of course!" Blurp replied.

"I'm missing one of my eyes. Have you seen it?" I asked.

"Ah, yes. I mean, no. I mean, oh dear, I can't seem to remember," he said. "I have such a terrible memory." Poor guy.

Fumble's eyes lit up. "Hey Blurp, I have an idea! I'm heading to the volcano to visit Elder Furi because I heard he can help me become more graceful. I'll bet you a billion Rox he could also help you with your memory!" she said.

"You really think so?" Blurp asked.

"I do!" Fumble replied.

"I do too! Hey, maybe I'll get lucky and we'll find my missing eye along the way." What an exciting way to spend my weekend! I thought to myself.

Once Blurp had gathered his things, we were off. We swam past schools of Batty Bubblefish, through scummy tunnels, and finally found ourselves at shore, but we must have taken a wrong turn because we weren't at The Port. We were right smack in the middle of Screamington Swamp!

The air was muggy and thick. The Bleurch Trees groaned in the slight breeze, shifting creepily against the dreary sky. We could hear Bog Frogs croaking and Sticky Crickets chirping all around us.

"Do you hear that?" I asked my two traveling companions.

"I c-c-can hear the c-c-crickets and the f-f-frogs," Fumble stuttered. She looked scared. I realized my knees were shaking as a chill ran up my spine.

"No, I hear someone whistling," I explained.

"Yes, I hear it too!" Blurp said.

"Toot-toot-toot-toot! Whee-whee-whee-whee!" The mysterious notes echoed through Screamington Swamp. It sounded beautiful! Somehow it put me at ease.

"I think we should follow the sound," I said. "We're a little lost and whoever is whistling that beautifully is probably going to be a friendly face."

"I think it's coming from over that way," Fumble said.

We followed the voice through the icky sticky harsh marshes, careful not to step on any Bog Frogs. We came upon a clearing and there was Stanley the Songful SeaHorse! His back was to us as he continued the most beautiful whistling I'd ever heard. He must've heard us approaching because his tune turned into a pitiful off-key shriek.

"Hiya Stanley! You don't have to stop just because we showed up," I said.

SCREAMINGTON SWAMP

CAFE COUGH COUGH

CAFE COUGH COUGH

"Uh, hi Roary. Hey Fumble and Blurp. Nah, I'm done whistling."

"Why are you all the way out here in the creepy crawly Screamington Swamp?" Fumble asked, shuddering.

"I like to sing out here because it's so quiet, 'ya know? I mean, I can really let loose and not have to worry about anybody hearing me," he replied.

"But you can turn such an incredible tune," Blurp said. "Why wouldn't you want anybody to hear it?"

"For some strange reason any time I try to whistle for anybody, I freeze up and can't toot. I get super nervous!" Stanley explained.

"Well guess what, Stanley?" I said. "We are headed to the Volcano to see if Elder Furi can help Fumble be more graceful and help Blurp improve his memory. Maybe he can help you with your stage fright! We're going to need your help finding our way out of Screamington Swamp, anyway."

"Sure, I'll be glad to help. I would love to be able to get over my stage fright. Let's go!" he exclaimed.

With Stanley in the lead, we were off towards the Volcano. We splashed through the Boggle-Eye Lagoon, got a little bit lost in North Southville, and finally found our way to Café Cough Cough where we decided to stop for a bite to eat. Adventures sure do make a monster hungry! As we walked up to the entrance, I noticed Cali the Valley Mermaid sitting on a bench, and she was crying.

"Hi Cali, what's wrong?" I asked, taking a seat beside her.

"Hi Roary. Hi Fumble, Blurp, and Stanley," she sniffled. "I'm just like, so bummed out right now. I just helped three of my friends find dates to the Moshling Boshling tournament after-party."

"The Moshling Boshling tournament! I'd nearly forgotten about it. That's tomorrow! Also, I thought you luuuurved being a matchmaker," I said.

"I do, I totally do. It's just that, no matter how hard I try, my flashing matchmaker heart powers only work for others. I STILL don't have a date," she snuffled.

"Cheer up Cali," Fumble suggested. "Let's all share a few orders of Crispy Fried Batwings and Roarberry Cheesecake and we'll tell you all about the adventure we're on!"

"Okay," Cali agreed.

After lots of snacks, Toad Soda, and Blurp's rendition of the burped out-of-order ABCs, Cali was in good spirits again. She even agreed to come with us to the Volcano to get help from Elder Furi for her heart power issue.

"If anybody sees my missing eye, please let me know," I reminded everybody as we strolled up Main Street towards the Volcano. Everybody mumbled okay. Nobody was thinking about my missing eye because they were all preoccupied dreaming about how Elder Furi was going to help them. We had a real sense of hope as we trudged up Sludge Street.

"We're almost there!" Cali declared. It was true. I could already smell the smoldering magnificent magma.

"There's the Gatekeeper," Fumble said, pointing with her sea-tip. "Whoah, uh oh!" she yelped, as she tripped on a lava rock, tumbling into a somersault and landing in a big pile of bat droppings.

"Are you ok, Fumble?" Blurp asked, hurrying over to help her up and brush her off.

"Yeah, I'm fine," she replied, embarrassed. We were almost to the Gatekeeper, and I was starting to feel a little nervous.

"Greetings!" bellowed the Gatekeeper. "What brings you to the Volcano?"

"H-h-hello Gatekeeper," I said. "We're here to see the great wise Elder Furi. We need some help with a few things."

"Only Super Moshis are allowed inside," he boomed.

"Oh, please, please let us inside," Fumble pleaded, looking extra pitiful since she'd just been face-down in bat droppings. Her bag had slumped to the ground and its contents had spilled everywhere. The Gatekeeper's eyes were fixed on something in her bag.

"Is that a jar of Octopus Spit from Potion Ocean?" the Gatekeeper asked.

"Yes, it sure is," Fumble responded.

"I will allow you to enter if you rub the soothing Octopus Spit on my ears. The lava mist up here makes them itchy and Octopus Spit is the only thing that brings me relief," he said.

"Of course!" Fumble said, as she set to work spreading the gooey stuff on his ears.

"Ahhhh, that's better!" he said, sighing with bliss. "You may enter now."

The door to the Volcano opened with a spectacular show and we went inside. Elder Furi greeted us with a wave of his staff.

"Greetings. I've been expecting you," said Elder Furi.

"Hello Elder F-f-furi. We're here bec-" I started.

Elder Furi interrupted, and said, "I'm glad you're here. I need your help."

"Oh, sure," I said. "But we're actually here to see you because we need help too."

"I will help you after you've helped me," he said.

"What can we do?" Fumble asked.

"As you may already know, the Moshling Boshling tournament is tomorrow. I need you to assist my Super Moshi crew to get the festivities set up down at the Firebowl."

"OMG, lots of my friends will be there. I can't believe we like, totally get to help out with this!" Cali shrieked.

Fumble did an awkward happy dance and Blurp had blown up with excitement.

"The Super Moshis will meet you there first thing in the morning," Elder Furi explained.

"Okay, Elder Furi. We will see you tomorrow!" I said.

On our way out, Fumble gave the Gatekeeper a final ear-scratch and we trekked up to Stumpy Peak. I figured it'd be a great place to set up camp for the night. It also happened to have a great view of The Firebowl. We roasted Garlic Marshmallows, told spooky stories, and played Go Fishies with Fumble's deck of cards until it was time for slumber.

"Did you see that?" Fumble asked. "A shooting star! Everybody make a wish."

"I know what I'm wishing for," Cali said.

"Me too," said Blurp and Stanley at the same time. They mumbled something about a jinx and then everybody was fast asleep and snoring.

The sun rose over The Firebowl and it looked like it was on fire. There was something in the air that morning. I could tell it was going to be a good day.

"Rise and shine, friends!" I said. "It's the big day!"

We marched down the mountain, excited and proud to help Elder Furi. When we got there, a group of Super Moshis were waiting for us.

"Hello! Elder Furi said you'd be here. There's a lot of work to do, so we hope you're up for the challenge," a dashing caped Diavlo said.

"Of course. What should we do first?" I asked.

"Elder Furi is giving a speech to kick off the games. I need you to write out the speech on some cue cards, and I'll need one of you to hold them up for him when he goes up there," the Diavlo said, handing Blurp a marker and lots of poster boards.

"Also, Avril Le Scream is ill today so we don't have anybody to sing the Monstro City Anthem. I need you to find us a singer, and quick!" the Diavlo said. "Plus, the lighting system is all tangled up in the rafters so I'll need one of you to get up there and untangle them. Time is of the essence!"

We were on a mission. Blurp set to work writing out Elder Furi's cue cards and Cali, Fumble, Stanley and I headed over to the stage.

"Stanley, since you're the most musical of all of us, why don't you find someone to take Avril Le Scream's place?" I suggested.

"Ok, Roary. I'll do my best!" Stanley replied, and went off on his quest.

We walked past the Moshling Boshling contenders who were stretching and drinking Craterade in preparation for the big game. A group of Stunt Penguins were gathered in a circle making a fuss over something. Cali, Fumble and I went over to investigate. DJ Quack was in the middle. They were arguing over who would go first in the tournament, and DJ Quack was obviously losing the battle. Cali, who HATES to see anybody fighting, elbowed her way inside the circle.

"Hey you guys!" she shouted. "Does it really matter who goes first? Won't you all end up at the same place in the end?" She looked over at DJ Quack, who was suddenly starry-eyed.

"Hi Cali," DJ Quack said sheepishly. "I guess you're right. If these bullies wanna go first, they can. I'll be the bigger bird," he shrugged. "By the way, do you have a date to the after-party? I'd love it if you'd come with me."

Cali's heart began to flash and her cheeks turned pink. "Like, totally!" she said. "I gotta go help my friends with something so I'll meet up with you later. Good luck in the games!"

When we got to the stage, it was clear we'd have to do some major maneuvering to get the lighting fixtures untangled. But how were we supposed to get up there?

"I have an idea," I announced. "Fumble, you're small, so I think you're the one with the best chance of fixing this. Let's borrow the giant slingshot from the Moshling Boshling arena and fling you up there."

Cali asked her new friend DJ Quack to let us borrow the slingshot. He even helped us carry it over to the stage. Once we had it steady, we hoisted Fumble into it. I pulled it back with all my strength and Fumble was airborne, somersaulting mid-air and landing haphazardly on the rafters.

"Uh oh, whoa!" Fumble cried out, as she almost fell off the narrow rafter.

"Just go slow, Fumble!" I yelled up at her. "I know you can do it!"

We all watched as she slowly made her way across the rafter and over to the tangled cords. She carefully unscrambled them in a matter of minutes.

"Ok, they're good to go now!" she said. Suddenly panic hit her face.

"Uh oh. How am I going to get down?"

"Can you grab that loose cord over there?" Cali asked. "You should be able to use it to swing down."

"Ok, I'll try it." Fumble said. She grabbed the loose cord, paused, and took a deep breath. Then she swooped down and swung out onto the stage. She looked like a trapeze artist! She even nailed the landing.

"Good job, Fumble!" I told her. "That was incredible."

"Thanks Roary!" she said. "We'd better get that slingshot back to the arena and check in on Blurp and Stanley."

When we found Blurp, he was shuffling the cue cards around with a worried look on his face.

"Oh dear," he said. "I'm worried these aren't in the right order."

"Let me see," I said, taking them and looking through them. "These are correct! Well done, Blurp."

"Thanks. Can someone else hold them up for Elder Furi when he gets on stage? I'm afraid I'll forget the order and mess it up," he said.

"I can't," Fumble said. "I have to watch over the lighting equipment to make sure they don't get tangled again."

"I like, totally would, but I definitely need to get a good seat to watch DJ Quack in the games," Cali explained.

"I can't either because I need to take notes for The Daily Growl," I said. "Looks like you're going to have to do it. I know you can!"

"Ok," Blurp agreed. He didn't sound so sure of himself. Stanley rushed over, looking panicked.

"Hi everybody. We have a slight emergency. I haven't been able to find anybody to sing the Monstro City anthem yet, and the show starts in five minutes!"

"Stanley, it'll be ok," I said. "If there's nobody else, then YOU will have to do it. The games can't go on without our anthem being played first. It's a known fact."

"Well, I suppose I could give it a try. But I'm not promising anything. You know what happens when I try to perform in front of people," he said.

"You'll do great," I said as I nudged him towards backstage.

I took my seat in the front row and waited for the show to begin. The lights dimmed and Stanley bounced onto the stage. He took a deep breath, and began to whistle. At first it was a little off-key, but he soon found his tune and wowed the crowd with his stunning warble of the Monstro City Anthem. I looked to my right and Buster Bumblechops even had a tear in his eye! After the last whistled note, the crowd burst to their feet in applause. He was amazing! Stanley looked shocked as he realized they were all standing up for him. He took a modest bow and bounced off stage.

The lights dimmed again and Elder Furi approached the podium.

"It is with great honor that I announce the third annual Moshling Boshling tournament," Elder Furi announced. "Three years ago today..." And he went on to describe the early days of the tournament.

At the end of his speech, Elder Furi said, "I have a few friends I'd like to thank. You see, Fumble came to see me yesterday because she wanted help being more graceful. But we wouldn't be here today if it weren't for her. She swooped up to the rafters and fixed our lighting problem, and she did it all with the grace of a trapeze artist.

"Blurp wanted my help in getting a better memory. But he's actually been able to remember the right order for my speech's cue cards, and he held them up in the correct sequence.

"Stanley had a bad case of stage fright, but wasn't he incredible in front of everybody here today?

"And Cali, who thought her matchmaking skills could only be used for others, found out today that she can in fact use her flashing heart powers for herself.

"Roary Scrawl however, is still missing his lost eyeball so if anybody finds it, please turn it in to the lost and found."

The crowd erupted in applause, and it was finally time for the games to begin. We were all on the edge of our seats as Moshlings were catapulted across the arena. The gold medal went to Peppy the Stunt Penguin and DJ Quack brought home the silver. After the tournament was over, we met up backstage.

"Can you believe what just happened?" I asked.

"No, it's just incredible!" Fumble said. "Hey Roary, I want you to have these as a special thank you for everything you've done to help." She handed me her deck of cards.

"Thanks, Fumble! These are really great," I said, hugging her.

Blurp tugged my arm. He was holding something out to me. It was my missing eye!

"Thanks, Blurp!" I said, popping it back in. "How'd you find it?"

"I finally remembered where I saw it last. It was in my pocket this whole time!" he explained.

"Hey, I think it's time for the after-party," Cali interrupted.

"Let's go!" Stanley said.

It was a party to remember, for sure. DJ Quack and Cali won the dance-off contest against a bunch of Stunt Penguins, Stanley led everybody in a round of scary-oke, and Blurp burped the ABCs...in the right order! Even Elder Furi came out and did his famous dance move, the Super Moshi Slide.

It's incredible how an ordinary day at The Port ended up being an amazing adventure, and how sometimes the things we need are with us the whole time (maybe just in someone's pocket)!

HOW TO PLAY GO FISHIES

Players: 2 or more

Deck: Full deck of Moshlings & Glumps

Deal: The entire deck

Object of the game: To get rid of all cards in your hand

Wild Cards: The Glumps. Can be used for any category

Categories: Moshling sets, i.e. Birdies, Dinos, Foodies, etc.

Game play:

Player 1 asks, "Do you have any Beasties?"

Player 2 either hands over their Beastie cards or says "Go Fishies!" if they DON'T have any Beasties in their hand.

Once a player has gotten all four of a Moshling set, they should lay them down in separate piles face up in front of them so everybody can see which set it is.

If a wild card has been used to complete a set, the other player may play the remaining cards from the category on that pile.

The first player to lay all their cards down is the winner.

BLURP'S MEMORY GAME

Players: 1 or 2

Deck: Monster cards only

Object of the game: To have the most matched sets

Game play:

Shuffle the deck and lay them out in a grid, face down. Players take turns flipping pairs of cards over. On each turn, the player will first turn one card over, then a second. If the two cards match, the player removes the two matching cards and puts them in a pile in front of them. If the cards don't match, the player turns them back over and it's the other player's turn. Continue to play until all the matches have been made. The winner will have the most matched sets.

HOW TO STUMP A GLUMP

Do you know what I like to do after an arrrghsome adventure? I like to go down to Tyra's Spa for a little argh and argh. There's nothing like a gloopy goo mask to make this monster feel like a new guy. Plus, Tyra gives me a discount.

"Hi Roary," Tyra said when I arrived. "You want your usual treatment today?"

"Yes please!" I replied. Tyra washed my face and applied the facial goo.

"We'll just let that sit for a few minutes," she said. I sat back in my chair and opened a magazine.

"Achoo!" I sneezed. "Ah-ah-ACHOO!"

"Gesundheit!" Tyra said. I'd never sneezed so hard in my life! The facial goo tickled my eyes. Something was NOT right. I ran over to rinse off the goo and felt immediate relief.

"That was definitely NOT my regular treatment," I said. "Let me see the bottle."

"Sure, here you go," she said, handing it over.

It looked normal enough, but when I looked closer I could

see that the label had been haphazardly slapped on. I ripped off the label and the bottle underneath said "Pepperbomb Foam – Do Not Apply to Face." I heard a muffled laugh coming from one of the drawers. I looked at Tyra. She'd heard it too and her eyes were wide with surprise.

I raced over and threw open the drawer and a Glump jumped out. It was Squiff! Squiff's face scrunched up and he ripped a Squiffy Stinkbomb right in the middle of the spa. All of the other customers gagged and ran outside with gloopy goo still on their faces. I lunged after Squiff but he got away and got out the front door.

"We gotta get out of here," I said to Tyra, who was in shock that she'd lost all of her customers for the day. I was feeling woozy from the fumes.

"My precious spa reeks!" she yelped, propping the front door open.

Monsters filled the street, their faces dripping with gloopy goo. Luckily they had gotten the real stuff and not the Pepperbomb Foam. Everybody was angry and they were yelling at Tyra. She looked over at me, panicked.

"I know you never wanted to give away the secret about Tyra's Rejuvenating Skin Goop, but I think this might be a good time," I whispered to her. Her eyebrows went up in thought and she finally nodded in agreement.

"Listen up everyone!" she announced. "I know you're all angry about having to leave so quickly with your goo masks still on. But I have good news, believe it or not. Tyra's Rejuvenating Skin Goop is edible! It includes Swirlberry extract and whipped cream." The crowd got quiet. A Katsuma licked some off of its face.

"Yum!" he said, licking the rest off. The rest of the monsters in the crowd did the same, and the crowd soon erupted in maniacal laughter.

"Good thing you didn't tell them it's also made with Tickly Feather essential oil," I whispered to Tyra and winked. The monsters were laughing uncontrollably. My ears perked up though because I could hear something in the distance. "Hey, do you hear that?"

"It sounds like something's going on over on Main Street," Tyra said.

"I'm going to go check it out," I said.

"I'm going to see what I can do about airing out the spa!" she added, using an old newspaper to fan the doorway to the spa.

WELCOME TO MONSTRO CITY

GROSS ERY STORE

OPEN

MOSHLING SEEDS

YUKEA

The commotion grew louder as I approached Main Street. Shoppers were slipping and sliding all around outside of Moe's shop. Some sort of gooey green stuff was all over the sidewalk.

"Excuse me, but what's going on?" I asked a Poppet.

"Hi Roary. It's crazy in there!" she said. She had green bubbles stuck in her fur. "I just needed an Arm Chair to go with my new Foot Table and, well... It's just madness! See for yourself."

I pushed my way through the front door and couldn't believe all of my eyes. Customers were slipping and sliding all around the shop and there were bubbles everywhere. Ooof! Something hit my leg. It was Moe Yukky and he was sprawled out on the ground. His foot was stuck in a mop bucket and he'd just slid across the floor.

"Roary, you've got to help me," he pleaded. "Glumps broke in here this morning and completely wrecked my shop!"

"What is all of this?" I asked.

"Green soap!" Moe cried. "It's everywhere!"

"Well, you always said you were the CLEANEST monster," I said, helping him to his feet. "Now there's proof."

"Very funny, Roary," Moe said, tugging at the bucket on his foot. *Splat!*

27

He fell again. The bucket rolled across the floor and another monster that was mid-skid tripped over it and tumbled into the shelves, knocking accessories onto the floor.

"Did you hear that, Moe?" I asked. "There's something in that pile of suds."

"You're right!" he agreed.

"Shhh," I whispered, sneaking up to the soapy mound. Just as I was about to pounce, I slipped and fell face-first into the bubbles. Fabio jumped out and nipped me with a Triple Tooth TerrorBite. *Chomp!* As quickly as he bit me, he had chomped his way out the back door.

"Are you okay?" Moe asked. "What the heck is going on?"

"The Glumps are taking over Monstro City," I explained as I rubbed my freshly-chomped arm. "They were causing trouble over at Tyra's Spa earlier, and now this."

"But it doesn't make sense," said Moe. "They're usually not this clever."

"You're right. Something's up. I'm going to go check on Snozzle Wobbleson over at the Gross-ery store," I told him.

I pushed my way out to the street, slipping and sliding. The other monsters helped me. Finally I made it over to the Gross-ery store. I opened the door. *Thwack!* A Slop bucket nearly hit me in the face. The whole shop was covered in food. The floor was sticky with Toad Soda, Gloop Soup dribbled down the walls, and empty Slop buckets were all over the place.

Pirate Pong was behind the counter, chucking food at customers. I scanned the room for Snozzle and spotted him hunkered down in the corner. With one arm up to shield my face I made my way over to him.

"Are you okay?" I asked. "This is nuts!"

"Hi Roary. This has been going on all morning! My shop is a mess," Snozzle cried. "All of my customers are leaving."

"Glumps are all over town, creating pandemonium everywhere they go," I said. I took a deep breath, mustered up all the courage I could, stood up tall, opened my mouth to say "Pirate P," and a Mississippi Mud Pie hit me square in the face. That was the last straw. I wiped my face on my sleeve and lunged for Pirate Pong but he darted out of my grasp. I chased him all the way out the front door but he got away.

"I'm going to go check on Dewy at the DIY shop," I said to Snozzle, who was rocking back and forth, still hunched in the corner.

I made my way over to Sludge Street, dodging monsters who were

GROSS-ERY STORE

OPEN

running around crazily covered in various slime, gunk, or goo. When I got to the DIY shop, I noticed a plume of black smoke coming from inside. I poked my head inside and saw Dewy struggling with one of his inventions.

"Roary! You gotta help me dude," he yelped. His patented Turbo Jumbo Jet Engine-fueled Jelly Bean Sorter was bouncing all around the shop, knocking everything off of the shelves. I ducked as a plank flew across the room.

"Do you have any rope?" I asked. "Maybe we can tie it down somehow."

"Yeah dude. Lemme grab some from the back." He was gone for just a minute while I dodged the erratic mechanical beast. He came back with soap.

"ROPE, Dewy, not soap!" I yelled. He shrugged and went back. This time he brought a length of rope.

"Good," I said. "Now, throw me the other end." I don't know how we managed it, but between the two of us we got the machine tied down and Dewy was able to find the kill switch. The machine sputtered and wheezed as it shut down.

"That was close!" I said, as I propped my elbow up on the counter. I accidentally knocked something on the ground. "Oops, sorry," I said, retrieving it. My eyes almost popped out when I saw what it was—a remote control with the words "Jelly Bean Sorter" on it, with an on and off switch. "Umm, Dewy? Has this been here the whole time?"

"Derr, oops," Dewy shrugged. "I forgot I had that."

"How did the jelly bean sorter go out of control in the first place?" I asked, taking deep breaths to keep my head from exploding.

"It was Bruiser," Dewy explained. "That lousy Glump came in here and was going all crazy with a bunch of Scarface Smashes and Scowling ScrimScrams. I figured I could use the Jelly Bean Sorter to get him to jet but he grabbed it and used a hammer to make it go all haywire. That's when you came in."

"Is Bruiser still h...?" A cackle floated out of the shelves. Dewy and I gave each other terrified glances. I tip-toed over to where the laugh came from. Zing! Bruiser came crashing down with a waterfall of ball bearings. I slipped and fell as Bruiser leaped over my face and out the door.

"Look at this huge mess, man," Dewy said, as he sat down behind the counter, tilted back in his chair, and opened a copy of Hammer Times. "Total bummer, but I'll clean it up later."

"I'm going to see if I can figure out this Glump problem. See ya later," I said as I left.

What was going on? Dewy was always flaky, but I'd never seen the Glumps so clever. They even seemed faster than normal! I began to think maybe a sinister force was behind this.

Thunk! I tripped on something. It was a candy package that said "Smart Tarts," and was covered in Burbling Gurgling Gobstopper drool. A Glump scurried across my path and snatched the Smart Tarts before I could stop it. It was Freakface, and he left a trail of Gobstopper drool behind him.

I decided the best thing to do was to track the trail. I had to get to the bottom of this. I followed it past shrieking monsters inside the Ice Scream shop, hysterical customers at the New Houses shop, and narrowly missed a mob of angry art aficionados at the Googenheim.

Finally I found the end of the drool trail at the entrance to the Candy Cane Caves. "Of course," I said aloud. "Only Sweet Tooth could be behind this. That explains the Smart Tarts!" I spun around to head back to town when I felt a candy cane around my neck. "Greetings, Roary," a sickenly sweet voice said. "How sweet of you to visit." I turned around to find Sweet Tooth at the other end of the candy cane.

SMART TARTS

"H-h-hello Sweet Tooth," I stammered, easing out of the candy crane's grip. "I was just strolling by, that's all. I'll be on my way now."

"How do you like the new and improved Glumps?"

"Th-th-they're so much smarter, and even more mischievous than normal," I said.

"That's right. Soon CLONC will take over Monstro City for good. Why don't you go write an article about how CLONC is going to rule supreme. Even your Super Moshis won't be able to beat us this time."

"Erm, okay," I said, backing away quickly. "I'll go do that right now." Sweet Tooth sure was creepy! On my retreat back to Monstro City my mind was spinning. Something had to be done, but what? Maybe the Super Moshis could help! I texted my Super Moshi friends, Moe, Dewy, Snozzle and Tyra and told them to meet me at The Daily Growl office in ten minutes. When I got there, they were all waiting for me.

"At least the Glumps haven't taken over my office," I said, hopefully. I held up a Smart Tarts wrapper. "The Glumps are eating these, and I'm pretty sure they're getting them from Sweet Tooth. Does anybody have an idea of how to get the Glumps to go away?"

"If only there was a way to trick the Glumps into giving up their Smart Tarts habit!" A brave looking Super Moshi Poppet said.

"Taking candy away from a Glump is no easy task," said Moe. "Anyway, who would want it after a Glump has had it? Bleck."

"Maybe we don't need to take anything away," A caped young Furi said. "But get them to eat something else."

"Yeah! If only we could trick them somehow," Tyra said.

"Like, what if we put a Smart Tarts label on a package of Dumbdrops? Then the Glumps will go back to being dumb again," I suggested.

"Now we're talkin'!" exclaimed Dewy.

"Dewy, you go pick up some Dumbdrops, and be sure to get the permanent-acting kind," I said. "The rest of us will get to work making fake Smart Tarts labels."

I got out my art supplies and we set up shop making Smart Tart labels. Soon, Dewy came back with an armload of Dumbdrops.

"Good job," I said, holding a pack of Dumbdrops, amazed that he'd gotten the correct kind. "Once they've eaten these, the Glumps will go back to being dumb for good and the Smart Tarts will lose their effect."

"We'll finally have peace and quiet, and no more messes." Moe said thoughtfully.

"Let's finish getting these

wrapped up and then we'll set them around town for them to find," I said.

"Wait a minute, you guys," Tyra said, holding a Dumbdrops wrapper. "It says here that for the Dumbdrops' effects to be permanent, a slight thump to the head must be administered."

"Let me see that," I said, taking it from Tyra. "It goes on to say that if the thump hasn't been administered before one hour's time, the effect will wear off completely."

"We've got some Glumps to thump!" Dewy yipped.

We headed outside with pockets full of our tricky sweets and planted them on every corner where Glumps would be sure to find them. Then we crouched behind a hill to take in the action. First one Glump found a pile and gobbled up some Dumbdrops, and before we knew it the entire street was covered in Dumbdrop-devouring Glumps! Soon enough, they'd all lost the smart twinkle in their eyes.

"Okay friends, we have exactly one hour to thump all of these Glumps!" I said. "Let's get em!"

Tyra thumped a Glump with a great *"Hiyahh!"* Moe thumped the next one with a medium sized *"Pow!"* Dewy decked a third with a DIY *"Doink!"* We were so busy thumping Glumps we didn't notice

the scent of licorice in the air. A shadow passed over us and a chill ran up my spine. Something was NOT right.

"Silly monsters," a voice bellowed from above. I looked up and saw Sweet Tooth coming down from the clouds wearing a Marshmallow Puffed Jet Pack. Smart Tarts rained down onto the street and into greedy Glumps' mouths from Sweet Tooth's hands. "Eat up, my little Glumps, so you can get back to work!"

As the Glumps munched away, I looked up and said, "Sorry Sweet Tooth. "They've all been given permanent Dumbdrops, so your Smart Tarts won't work on them anymore!"

"What!?!" Sweet Tooth cried. "My precious Smart Tarts neutralized? All my evil work was for nothing. Nothing!" What happened next was something none of us could have anticipated. Sweet Tooth started eating the Smart Tarts, one after another until there were no more. A crazed look entered Sweet Tooth's eyes and then the unbelievable happened.

The more Sweet Tooth ate, the larger Sweet Tooth got, blowing up like a balloon. Some Dumbdrops must've gotten mixed up in that jelly-coated belly causing an explosive reaction. Pretty soon all we could see were those sugary shoes. And then, suddenly, *Buuuuurp!*

It was the biggest belch I'd ever heard, and it blew Sweet Tooth all the way back to the Candy Cane Caves.

"We probably won't be seeing Sweet Tooth anytime soon," said Dewy, absentmindedly popping a Dumbdrop into his mouth.

"Dewy! Don't!" I shouted. But it was too late. He'd already chewed it up and swallowed it.

"Derr, it's okay. I eat 'em all the time." Dewy said. My jaw dropped in disbelief. Well that certainly explained a lot about Dewy!

"That was so exciting," Tyra said. "I'm just glad Sweet Tooth won't be bothering us anymore."

"Yeah, I'll bet that tummy ache is going to last for a long time," I said. "Thanks, Super Moshis, for helping us today."

"It's quite alright," the Super Katsuma said. "It's what we're here for. We keep CLONC at bay so you can play!"

"Heh. I wish I could play. THIS monster has to get back to work!"

HOW TO PLAY THUMP A GLUMP

Players: 2 or more

Deck: Full deck of Moshlings and Glumps

Deal: The entire deck

Object of the game: To get all the cards

Game play:

Shuffle and deal the entire deck equally between the players. Everybody holds their cards in a face-down hand. Going around the table clockwise, each player discards the top card from their hand face up in a middle pile. When someone plays a Glump card, the first player to thump it wins the entire middle pile. Play continues starting with the player on the left to the one who won the cards. The object of the game is to get all of the cards. When a player runs out of cards, they are out of the game but can still thump Glumps and get back into the game by winning the pile.

Don't look at a card before you play it, everybody should see the card at the same time as you play it. It's best to turn the card over in the center of the table above the pile so everybody has a fair chance to see the card.

If several people thump at the same time, the person whose hand is underneath and in contact with the card is the winner of the cards.

If a player thumps a non-Glump card, the player who thumped incorrectly has to give the top card of their own pile face down to the person who played the card that was wrongly thumped. That person adds it to the bottom of their own pile.

When one player has all the cards, that player wins. Or you can play with a time limit and at the end of that time the player with the most cards wins.

THE SCHOOL OF DROOL

After all the excitement of the Glump takeover, I was ready to get back to my normal everyday life as Editor in Chief of The Daily Growl. My big job for the week was to judge the Beanie Blob contest. Monster owners all over Monstro City sent in drawings for new Beanie Blobs and I had to pick the best one. Not an easy job for someone who's not a Beanie Blob expert! I figured I'd go to the Beanie Blob makers themselves over at The School of Drool where apprentice Blob Sloggers stitched together the beanies. I'd never been there and was excited to see what it was like, so I hopped on my trusty scooter.

When I finally got there, the building towered over me, blocking the sun. *Creeeeeak!* The door squeaked open and I found myself in an empty dusty hallway. Above me was a dirty, cobweb-covered chandelier. The wallpaper was peeling off and the floor groaned in protest as I stepped forward. Just as I got to the end of the hallway, an icy hand clamped down on my shoulder.

"Not so fast!" a voice growled.

I spun around on my heels and found myself under the scowling face of a very tough looking Poppet. She was wearing an olive green track suit with the words "Number One Blob Slogger" embroidered on the sleeve and her name, "Rue Crueljester" on the front. A whistle hung loosely around her neck and she was holding a megaphone.

"Where do you think you're going?" she demanded.

"Hello, Rue," I read from her jacket. "I'm Roa-"

"I know who you are," Rue interrupted. "You write that ridiculous excuse for a newspaper called The Daily Scowl," she said.

"It's actually The Daily Gro-" I started.

"I don't care what it's called. So you're here for one of your little stories? Follow me," Rue commanded.

I followed her brisk walk through corridor after corridor until we came to a room that was different than all the others. This room wasn't dusty or grimy, it was spotless, and lined with cases filled with trophies.

"These are my regional and national trophies from the Blob Slogging Championships. This room just smells like winning," Rue said proudly.

"Wow," I said, taking in the sheer volume of trophies. "You sure have a lot of them!"

"That's what hard work, no Slop breaks, and long hours will get you," she said sternly.

"This one is really neat," I said, reaching out to touch it.

"Don't touch them!" Rue yelled. "I don't have sloggers polishing them for hours just to get slimy fingerprints all over them."

I knew I was going to have to speak up if I was ever going to complete my mission and find an apprentice Blob Slogger to help me, or else I'd be hearing about Rue Crueljester's epic wins all afternoon.

"I'm here today because I need an apprentice Blob Slogger to come out to The Daily Growl office and help me judge the Beanie Blob art contest," I explained.

"Well I'm sorry for not being sorry for what I'm about to tell you, but I need all of my apprentices to reach quota this week," Rue said.

"Oh, please, Rue?" I begged.

"What's in it for me?" she asked, with one eyebrow raised.

"Err, umm, I could write a story about how you're the best Blob Slogger in all of Monstro City?" I offered.

Rue's face lit up and I could almost hear the wheels spinning in her head. "Well, in that case, I suppose I could spare just one apprentice for a while," she said. "Come with me," she ordered, and pulled me by my sleeve down a series of hallways.

She shoved open a heavy metal door with the words "Apprentice Blob Slogger Station" crossed out and the word "SERVANTS" scrawled across it. Once through the door, we were standing at the top of a metal set of stairs. Down below stretched the enormous factory where the Blob Sloggers stitched together Beanie Blobs.

There was a station in the back corner where they were sewing together the outer shells for the blobs; next to that, a station for sewing on the eyes. There was a station for striping, a station for spotting, and a station for free-hand painting. They were singing as they worked.

In the very back corner I noticed a Zommer who wasn't singing. He looked different than all the rest of the workers, with neon green hair, orange sneakers, and pins and stickers all over his shirt. His employee badge said "Drool 33."

"Who's that back there in the corner with the green hair?" I asked.

"SLOGGING DAY AND NIGHT,
WE NEVER PUT UP A FIGHT;
WE ALL ACT THE SAME
TO GO DOWN IN BLOB SLOGGER FAME.
WE AIM TO PLEASE
SO RUE DOESN'T SET LOOSE THE FLEAS;
WE LIVE TO WORK
WHILE RUE CRUELJESTER LURKS."

"Oh, don't mind him. He's a sloppy freakshow. Plus, he's the worst Blob Slogger I've ever met. He sews the eyes on backwards! One time he even stitched a blob to himself," she said. "Clearly not champion-qualified," Rue sniffed.

"What's his job?" I asked.

"I keep him back in the corner sorting the button-eyes so he can't disturb the rest of the serv-err, sloggers," she said.

"Can I go meet him?" I asked.

"I don't know why you'd want to do that. I'd rather eat a Beanie Blob for breakfast than deal with him," Rue sneered. "I'll be in my trophy room. Let me know who you end up taking, eyeball boy."

I headed down the stairs and made my way through the maze of Blob stations. The other workers didn't even look up they were so focused on their work. Despite their singing, they were all frowning. What a miserable bunch, I thought.

"Three hundred and seventy-nine, three hundred and eighty..." The green haired Zommer counted out loud, while plopping button eyes into a big barrel.

"Hello there. Sorry to interrupt you, but I really like your hair," I told him.

"Who, me?" he said, looking around as if to make sure I was talking to him. "Oh, thanks." He was obviously a bit frazzled.

"What's your name?" I asked.

"Rocky. Rocky Octave. And you're Roary Scrawl. I LOVE reading The Daily Growl but it's hard to get ahold of around this place. Rue Crueljester lets us have just one copy between all of us, and since I'm way back in this corner I usually get it last. Plus, the other apprentices think I'm a weirdo because of the way I look."

"I don't think you're a weirdo," I told him. "I really like your style. You look like a total rock star!"

"You really think so? I've always dreamed of being a rock star like Riff Sawfinger. He shreds the guitar!"

"Hey, I'm judging the Beanie Blob art contest and need a Beanie Blob expert assistant. Could you help me out?" I asked.

"Well, I'm not really an expert, Roary," he said. "I'm the worst Blob Slogger here."

DROOL 33

"Yeah, but I can tell by your fabulous flair and neon green hair that you've got a creative eye, and that's just what I need," I explained. "But don't worry, I'll give the eye back to you!" I said with a wink.

RUE CRUELJESTER

Shelby Wax

"Rue Crueljester would NEVER let me leave," he moaned.

"Well, it won't hurt to ask!" I waited until he'd finished his eye-sorting task and then we headed up to the trophy room to confront Rue.

The trophy room smelled of fresh Shelby Wax. Rue was busy polishing her trophy collection.

"Hey Rue," I said. "I'd like to take Rocky Octave with me to judge the Beanie Blob contest."

"I thought I smelled a loser," she puffed. "Go ahead and take him. He's pretty much useless. Maybe he can sort out YOUR eyes, Roary. Heh. They're all jumbled all over your head. You look like some kind of freakish eyeball porcupine. And what's up with that bowtie?"

(I had to admit, even though that was really mean, it was kinda funny. Hey, if you can't laugh at yourself, what can you laugh at? That's my motto anyway.)

"Ok, we'll see you soon." I said.

When we got outside I gave Rocky my spare helmet and we rode back to town on my scooter. When we got to my office, I left him at my desk to look over the Beanie Blob art entries and went outside to make a call from my Eye-Phone.

"Hey there," I said when Simon Growl answered. "I was wondering if any of the musical artists you manage might be free to spend some time with me at The Daily Growl office?"

"Oh hello, Roary. I'll interrupt my very busy schedule here to take a look. The Groanas Brothers are on tour, as are the Pussycat Poppets. Let me think for a minute. Ah yes. Avril Le Scream and Riff Sawfinger are back from their tour with The Fizzbangs. gave them comments on their last concert yesterday, so they should be in the rehearsal studio. What do you neeed?"

BEANIE BLOB FOR YOU!
Rocky's Blog Slogger number will get an exclusive Beanie Blob added to your monster inventory! The answer is your secret code, but remember do not use spaces!

"I just met a very special apprentice Blob Slogger over at The School of Drool, and I think he'd lose his mind jamming with them. Erm, hopefully not literally!" I said.

"Fine. I'll send them over as soon as possible," he said, clicking off the phone.

Rocky was going to luuuurve this surprise! I went back inside and Rocky had already chosen a winner from the contest. It was a Beanie Blob that had a bunch of colorful musical notes on it.

"Good choice, Rocky!" I said.

"Thanks. I love music. There's only so many times you can hear the Blob Slogger song – I mean, Rue isn't exactly a musical genius. I wish we could listen to some actual music."

"Did you hear that?" I asked. "I think I just heard someone knocking on the door downstairs. I'm going to go see who it is."

I opened the door and Riff Sawfinger was standing there with Avril Le Scream, next to a giant trunk with stickers all over it.

"Hey Roary!" Riff said.

"Hello! Welcome to The Daily Growl office." I said. "Come on upstairs. I have someone very special I want you to meet."

"Sure!" said Avril, smiling.

The first thing Riff said when he saw Rocky was, "Rockin' hair, dude!"

Rocky spun around in my office chair, his eyes wide in shock. "Wow, Riff Sawfinger. And Avril Le Scream! OMG I can't believe you guys are here!"

"We heard that you were a really rad dude and that we should meet you." Riff said.

"Really?" Rocky asked.

"Yeah, Rocky." I said. "I was thinking we could have a jam session! Do you play any instruments?"

"I play the guitar sometimes, but I don't have one with me," he said.

"Don't worry. We brought a bunch of instruments with us. I'm sure we can even find something for Roary," Riff said.

"I can play the triangle!" I offered.

We had the most epic jam session ever. Riff sang his hit song, "Monstro City," with Avril on backup. Rocky kept up with them, and even managed a few solos. I kept the beat with my trusty triangle. Afterwards, I got out my lucky cards that Fumble had given me, and got ready for a game of DROOL - the monster game of deception.

"This was the best day ever!" Rocky said, shuffling the deck.

"Yeah it was a blast," said Avril.

Rocky frowned. "I'm just so sad I have to go back to The School of Drool and be a Blob Slogger again."

"It's really not a fun place." I explained to Riff and Avril. "The boss lady, Rue Crueljestor, is really mean. Plus, she doesn't let them listen to music while they work."

"Oh man, that's brutal," Riff said. "Doesn't she know that music makes monsters happy?"

"As far as she's concerned, Rue's happiness is all that matters. DROOL!" Rocky chimed in, calling me on my bluff of three twos.

I picked up the pile of cards begrudgingly. "Hey, have you ever wondered what would happen if you could somehow play music for the other apprentice Blob Sloggers?" I asked.

"That'd never happen." Rocky said. "Rue would never allow it."

"But what if we were sneaky about it?" I suggested. "What do you guys say? Want to stage an impromptu concert for The School of Drool tomorrow?"

"I'm in," said Avril.

"Me too. DROOL!" chirped Riff at Avril, who said she'd set down three tens.

The next day we had a fool-proof plan ready to set into motion. I had to distract Rue Crueljestor, while Rocky, Riff and Avril got set up on the metal staircase above the factory area. Then I needed to get Rue to the factory floor for the show of a lifetime!

We loaded up Simon Growl's extra tour bus with the equipment and were off to The School of Drool with our assignments. I figured Rue would be in her trophy room so I went there first. Sure enough, she was in there, polishing her trophies AGAIN.

"Hi Rue!" I said, cheerfully. "I would love to show you the article I'm working on about you, but I left it in your office."

"Well I want to see it, straight away!" she said.

"Ok, let's go!" I said.

When we got to her office, I noticed a bunch of plaques on her wall. I'd found the perfect distraction.

"What can you tell me about all those plaques?" I asked. "I might be able to use some of the info for my article all about you."

"Well, this one shows how I was the fastest Blob Slogger at The School of Drool back when I was still an apprentice," she said. "And this one..."

She went on and on and on about them all! I was SURRIOUSLY in there for like twenty minutes while she gabbed and I pretended to take notes.

"Wow, thanks for that very in-depth look at all of your awards and certifications." I said. "Do you think you could introduce me to some of your top producers?" I asked in my best reporter voice.

"Sure, newsboy," she said as she nudged me towards the factory floor. "Behold my empire...," Rue announced, pushing open the door. "Huh. What's that racket?" she growled, looking puzzled.

Rockin' tunes were coming from the top of the factory staircase. Avril Le Scream was singing a love song with Riff Sawfinger on backup. Rocky broke into a guitar solo worthy of a rock star, and really shredded it. I couldn't believe my eyes. The apprentice Blob Sloggers were all dancing and their once expressionless faces were beaming with joy. Somehow they were managing to work their stations at the same time.

"Look at them go!" Rue exclaimed. "I haven't seen them work that fast since I told them I was going to take away their fifteen minute Slop breaks if they didn't produce at twice their regular pace."

Rue was smiling and even tapping her foot to the tunes. Riff took the lead on the next song, an upbeat pop tune. By the time they played their last one, the apprentice Blob Sloggers had made so many Beanie Blobs that they covered the floor and were up to our knees. We were right smack in the middle of a Beanie Blob bog!

Riff whispered something to Avril and Rocky. They all grinned at each other and then dove off the staircase and into the huge pile of Beanie Blobs. All of the apprentices rushed over to cheer on the trio, and lifted them high above their heads. Beanie Blobs were flying everywhere and cheers and laughter filled the once dreary room.

"ALRIGHT EVERYBODY QUIET!" Rue yelled into her megaphone. The room got completely silent, the apprentices put everybody back down on the ground, and Rocky hung his head in defeat.

"Quiet-so I can congratulate Rocky on helping us become even MORE productive. I didn't think it was possible!"

Rocky looked up, shocked. "I-I don't know what to say," he stammered.

"For starters, you all can tell me what else you think we can do to be more productive," Rue said.

One of the apprentice Blob Sloggers raised his hand.

"Excuse me, M-M-Miss Rue. But I think we should have our Beanie Blob painters make murals in here. I get so tired of staring at the blank walls," the apprentice said.

"Yeah, and I'm tired of this boring uniform. Please can't we wear what we want without being sent to the eye-sorting corner?" another apprentice asked.

Rue looked down at her own drab outfit. "I suppose we could do with a bit more color," she confessed. "Now, let's get these Beanie Blobs boxed up! We've surpassed our quota for the week already! Everybody can go home early once we're done with that. Don't get used to me being nice-I've just used up my yearly allowance." Everybody cheered and got to work.

Avril, Riff, and I headed back to Monstro City. I had an article to write and Simon Growl said they had to get back to the music studio. I returned to The School of Drool a week later to see how they were doing. The sign on the building had been changed from "The School of Drool" to "The School of Cool." I snapped a photo of it for my article.

I pushed open the door and the first thing I noticed was the peeling wallpaper had been replaced by bright blue paint with yellow polka dots. Artwork decorated the walls and the chandelier had been cleaned up and now was sporting several SUPER hip Beanie Blobs. I made my way down the hallway and felt a familiar icy cold paw grab my shoulder.

SCHOOL OF COOL

"Roary!" Rue said. "Welcome to The School of Cool, man." She was wearing a bright red jumpsuit that said "World's Best Boss" on the sleeve. "Do you like my new outfit? The apprentices made it for me during their breaks this week."

"I LUUUURVE it!" I said. "How is everybody getting along?"

"Follow me, and I'll show you," she said. We walked through the brightly painted hallways back to the top of the metal staircase. I couldn't believe my eyes (all of them!) OR my ears!

Speakers belted out music from every corner. The factory floor looked like a rainbow since the apprentices were dressed in bright oranges, blues, purples, and pinks. Everybody was dancing, singing, and laughing as they worked. I tried to find Rocky but the Eye-Sorting corner was empty. I searched the crowd for his neon green hair but there were LOTS of apprentices with neon hair now, ranging from green to orange, purple and blue!

"Where's Rocky?" I asked Rue.

"He's in the trophy room," Rue said.

I couldn't believe it. After all Rocky had done to help The School of Drool, and Rue had him busy polishing her trophies. Hmph! We walked towards the trophy room, and my jaw dropped when I opened the door.

Rocky was inside, and there wasn't a trophy in site! The room had been converted into a DJ booth with a window that looked onto the factory floor.

"Hey Roary," Rocky said, shifting his headphones off one ear. "So maybe Blob Slogging wasn't my thing. But it turns out I'm an excellent DJ!"

"Wow," I said. "I can't believe how much better this place is."

"Thanks for believing in me, Roary," Rocky said.

"I could see that you already believed in yourself," I said. "It takes guts to be different, especially when people are hard on you. You

dared to be true to yourself, even if it meant you had to sort eyes in the corner. Speaking of eye sorting... I need to get back home. I've misplaced my eye again."

"About that article..." Rue said. "As you know, I believe in developing the skills of all my Blog Slave—err, Sloggers. Rocky merely modeled himself after my charming personality and made himself a winner just like me. That's the news fit to print, buddy! I'll be in my office if you need any more quotes," Rue said, as she walked out of the room.

"Ummm, yeah Rue, sure," I responded. Rocky and I exchanged glances and shook our heads. Some people never change!

Rocky smiled, and clicked on my favorite song, "Monstro City" by The Fizzbangs. I headed out the door, looking forward to whatever new adventures came my way today in Monstro City.

HOW TO PLAY DROOL

Players: 2 or more

Deck: Moshlings and Glumps

Deal: The entire deck

Object of game: To get rid of all your cards.

Game play:

Shuffle and deal all cards to the players. Select at random who should go first and continue clockwise.

In the middle is a discard pile that starts out empty. A turn consists of discarding one or more cards face down on the pile, and calling out their rank. The first player discards aces, the second, twos, the third, threes, and so on. After tens come Jacks, then Queens, then Kings, then back to aces, etc.

The name of the game is bluffing, so you don't actually have to play the rank you're calling. If it's your turn to discard eights, you may actually discard any card or mixture of cards. If you don't have any eights you will be forced to play some other card or cards.

Any player who suspects the card(s) discarded by a player don't match the rank called can challenge the play by yelling out "DROOL!" The challenged player must show everybody their discarded cards and one of two things happens.

If they are all of the rank that was called, the challenge is false and the challenger must pick up the entire discard pile.

If any of the played cards is different from the rank that was called, the challenge is correct and the person who played the cards must pick up the whole discard pile.

After the challenge is resolved, play continues in normal rotation: the player to the left of the one who was challenged plays and calls the next rank in sequence.

The first player to get rid of all their cards and survive any challenge resulting from their final play wins the game. If you play your last remaining card(s), but someone challenges you and the cards you played are not what you called, you pick up the pile and play continues.

GROSS GLUMP

Players: 2 to 8

Deck: Moshling & Glump cards, minus one Glump card

Deal: Remove one Glump card from the deck. Shuffle the deck and deal all cards as evenly as possible.

Object of the game: To get rid of all your cards and avoid being the Gross Glump

Game play:

First, players should organize their cards by pairs and place any pairs they have in their hands in a pile in the center of the table.

Then choose who will start play, which will be clockwise. The first player places their fanned-out hand face-down in front of the second player (to their left). The second player removes one card from the first player's hand. If the new card enables the second player to make a pair, then they should set their new pair down in the middle. Otherwise, player 2 would just keep it in their hand.

Next, player 2 places their fanned-out hand face-down in front of player 3 (to their left), who removes one card from player 2's hand. They will either make a match and discard in the center pile, or just keep the card in their hand. Play continues until one player is left with just one Glump card. That player is the Gross Glump!

DR. STRANGEGLOVE'S TAKE YOUR PICK TRICK

Deck: Moshlings and Glumps

Object of the trick: Amaze your friend by reading their mind!

Shuffle the deck and hold them so you can see the backs. Make sure that all cards are facing the same direction so that the word "Moshi" is right-side up. Once you've done that you're ready to start your trick.

Ask a friend to "pick a card, any card." When they remove the card, ask them to look at it and remember which card it is. Casually turn the deck in your hand so that it's facing the other way (so the word "Moshi" is upside down when you look at it). Ask your friend to put the card back into the deck, making sure that their card goes back in right-side up. Now you can shuffle the deck. Fan out the cards with the backs facing you and the fronts facing your friend. Find the card that's right-side up and that's the card your friend picked. Before you point it out, say "And shazam! Here's your card!"

Answer to clue on *The Daily Growl* page (p.2): THEFIZZBANGS   Answer to clue on page 48: DROOL33

THE MOSHLING BOSHLING TOURNAMENT

Deck: Just the Glumps, Techies, Ponies, and Fishies

Object of the trick: To get all the Moshling sets to "sit together"

Say, "The Glumps went to the Moshling Boshling Tournament." Now lay the four Glump cards in a row.

Say, "The Techies went to the tournament and chatted with the Glumps before it started." Now lay the four Techies cards so that the Glumps and Secrets are both visible.

Say, "The Ponies showed up and chatted with the Glumps and Techies before the tournament started." Now lay the four Ponies cards so that the Glumps, Secrets, and Ponies are all visible.

Say, "Then the Fishies arrived and chatted with the Glumps, Techies, and Ponies before it started." Now lay the four Fishies cards on top of the Ponies cards so that the Glumps, Techies, Ponies, and Fishies are all visible.

Say, "Now it's time for the tournament to begin, so all the Moshling return to their seats." Now turn all of the stacks over so they're face down.

Pick up the first stack and place it on top of the second stack. Then pick up the new, bigger stack and place it on top of the third stack. Pick up the new bigger stack and place it on top of the fourth stack.

Say, "Cut the cards by taking a group of cards off the stack and placing them on the table, then put the remaining cards on top of the stack. You can cut as many times as you like." Let the spectator cut the cards a few times, then deal the first four cards face-down next to each other. Then deal the next four cards on top of the first four cards, and so on, just like when you dealt them out the first time but this time they're face-down.

Say, "Okay, now they're all sitting together, enjoying the tournament." Turn them over, and you'll see that all the Moshling sets are "sitting together" in the same column!